Text Copyright © 1994 by Frances Thomas. Illustrations Copyright © 1994 by Ruth Brown
This paperback edition first published in 2003. The rights of Frances Thomas and Ruth Brown to be identified as the author and illustrator of this work have been asserted by them in accordance with the Copyright, Designs and Patents Act, 1988. First published in Great Britain in 1994 by Andersen Press Ltd. 20 Vauxhall Bridge Road, London SW1V 2SA. Published in Australia by Random House Australia Pty., 20 Alfred Street, Milsons Point, Sydney, NSW 2061.
All rights reserved. Colour separated in Switzerland by Photolitho, Zürich.
Printed and bound in Italy by Grafiche AZ, Verona.

10 9 8 7 6 5 4 3 2 1

British Library Cataloguing in Publication Data available.

ISBN 1 84270 226 2

This book has been printed on acid-free paper

Mr Bear & the Bear

Story by Frances Thomas
Pictures by Ruth Brown

Andersen Press • London

Everyone called him Mr Bear, though perhaps he had another name. "Cross as a bear," people said. Nobody smiled at him in the street, children stuck their tongues out behind his back. Dogs growled and cats ran away.

Mr Bear & the Bear

He had lived for many years in the big house on the hill.
Behind was a large garden with trees and a high wall all
around. Mr Bear grew older and crosser in the dark house.

One day he had to go to town to get his spectacles mended. The town was noisy and full of people.

The crowds pushed him this way and that, and he found himself in the town square with roundabouts and jugglers and stalls selling gingerbread and sugar plums.

A man held a stick and chain. On the other end of the
chain was a bear, with a ring through his nose. His mouth
was kept shut by a muzzle. There were shackles on his
back paws. He was smelly and his coat was matted
as an old rug. His eyes were dull and runny.

When the man poked him, the bear had to stand on his hind legs. The man poked again, and the bear jumped, lumbering from one foot to another. It looked as if he were dancing and all the people laughed and clapped their hands.

But Mr Bear could see that the bear did not dance for joy.
"Dance!" said the man. The bear danced and the
people clapped.

Mr Bear left the square and the town and went slowly up the hill to the dark house. He looked cross as he walked. "Cross as a bear," people said.

That night he could not sleep. He did not remember the music or the roundabouts, but he thought of the bear with the sad dull eyes.

Then he sat up in bed. He looked crosser than ever. But he had an idea.

Very early the next morning, he got his horse and wagon and set off for town. Almost no-one was about, except the street sweeper and the baker opening his shutters and yawning. But all the wagons and roundabouts had gone, all the striped tents and gingerbread stalls.

Mr Bear saw a small girl carrying water.

"Where did the fair go?" he asked.

"That way," she said, pointing.

Mr Bear did not thank her. The little girl shook her head. "Cross as a bear," she thought.

Mr Bear left the town. The sun rose in the sky, and the road was wide and dusty.

At midday he saw the man by the side of the road, eating a sausage. His horse was eating grass. And there in a cage, eating nothing at all, slumped the dirty old bear.

"I've come to buy your bear," said Mr Bear to the man.

The man laughed and took another bite of sausage. Mr Bear took out his purse, and showed the man a gold piece.

"The bear isn't for sale," said the man. Mr Bear showed him another gold piece. And another. The man yawned.

"I've had enough of bears anyway. Too cross. Take him. I'll stick to juggling in future."

They lifted the cage on to the wagon. The bear growled.
Mr Bear took apples from his bag and fed them to the bear.
The journey home was long and bumpy. When the bear
growled, Mr Bear gave him more apples. In that way they
got home, though by the time they did, it was nearly dark.

That night, in Mr Bear's woods, the bear slept well. Mr Bear had given him a strong sleeping potion. While he slept, Mr Bear took off the chain and muzzle. He broke the shackles. He chopped up the cage and burned it.

While the bear slept, he dreamed. He dreamed of the time long ago, when he had played in the hills with his mother, his brothers and sisters. He remembered splashing in the silvery water and catching fish. He remembered rolling in soft grass, and sniffing for ripe berries.

Then he dreamed of the time the hunters came. They took the bear and his brothers and sisters and sold them.

When he remembered this, it made him wake with an angry growl. Then he opened his mouth wide and yawned. He lifted up his head and stretched. There was no chain to jerk him back to the ground; no cold slippery cage, only soft, sweet grass. He stood up unsteadily, on his four paws. He could smell delicious water.

He took one step, then another. Still no chain stopped him. Nobody shouted at him or hit him. Into the stream he lumbered, and splashed, slowly at first, then faster. Cool water ran down his dry matted fur, his burning throat and into his sticky jammed-up eyes.

When he shook himself all over, he remembered how hungry he was. Across the garden, sitting quietly on the grass, was the man who had given him apples.
He liked apples.

And there was more: porridge, honeycomb and nuts.
The bear ate everything up. He had not eaten
such delicious things for a long time. He looked
at Mr Bear, who looked back at him. Mr Bear smiled.

More Andersen Press paperback picture books!

The Big Sneeze
by Ruth Brown

Betty's Not Well Today
by Gus Clarke

Dear Daddy
by Philippe Dupasquier

War and Peas
by Michael Foreman

Dilly Dally and the Nine Secrets
by Elizabeth MacDonald and Ken Brown

Sad Story of Veronica Who Played the Violin
by David McKee

Princess Camomile Gets Her Way
by Hiawyn Oram and Susan Varley

Lazy Jack
by Tony Ross

Bear's Eggs
by Dieter and Ingrid Schubert

Rabbit's Wish
by Paul Stewart and Chris Riddell

Frog and a Very Special Day
by Max Velthuijs

What Did I Look Like When I Was a Baby?
by Jeanne Willis and Tony Ross